PRINCE OF LUST

Lucien Burr

PRINCE OF LUST
Lucien Burr

Edited by Drew McBlain

Cover Art by Aresna Ada Villaneuva

Book Design by Lucien Burr

Ebook design by Lucien Burr

This book is a work of fiction and as such all characters and situations are fictitious. Any resemblance to actual people, places or events is coincidental.

Category (Adult Erotic Fiction)
Genre (Paranormal/ Romance / LGBT)

————

Foreword

Content Warnings:

Homophobia, slur usage, degradation, gore mention, blood, blood play, knife play, body horror, explicit sex scenes, religious themes, religious mockery

PROLOGUE

hame, guilt, disgust. I can name any number of things that drove me to the cloth.

When I spoke to my peers, my story never aligned with theirs. They described their love of God. The light. The various visions they received, or the whispering of angels urging them to do holy work, to commit themselves fully to our God above.

Not me.

If I was hearing anything at all, I was hearing the Devil.

Blasphemy before I've introduced myself? The scandal.

I am Don Alessandro: thirty-six, crinkled around the eyes, tall but soft in body. Who I am boils down to very little because I am meant to be a vessel of the Lord. Long ago, I gave up any chance of knowing myself.

Which is why I want to ruin my life, you see.

I am older. I am jaded. And I no longer think God is merciful.

———

The first lustful thought I had taught me the severity of shame: that in recognising my body and its desires, I would be condemned. I had said the wrong thing; I was a child, and I saw an older boy pulling water from a well in my village, bronze arms tense and straining as he pulled—and I compared him aloud to an angel.

I still remember the look on my mother's face, a disgust that was only dislodged when my father tried to beat desire out of my flesh. I became something else very quickly, which was quiet. The best defence is to say nothing incriminating at all.

Ever since then, the damned rot of shame had taken hold of me. It was insidious. I pride myself on being rather insightful; I have always been told my counsel was sound. Compassionate. Brilliant, even. But all that insight did for me was turn me around in circles. I knew where the shame came from and why I had it in me. Also, maybe, that God's test for me bordered on the cruel.

What didn't help me was that, in all my years of prayer and work and hope, nothing was enough to stop the dream.

I knew what I was. I knew what I wanted. I knew, in the eyes of the institution I had dedicated myself to, I was worth very little. I had been touched by the wrong force—that the Devil himself had corrupted me. Perhaps that was true. Perhaps he had. And perhaps I had been combating that influence for most of my life.

But where had shame gotten me?

I knew where it had sent me. Shame drove me to the church—sent me running like I was fleeing God's wrath itself. I knew if I were to linger in the world, then I would do the unthinkable.

I would fall in love with a man. I would touch him. I would love it.

. . .

Years after joining the monastery, I still loved it. Still craved it. But shame had such a hold on me—it had me leashed—that I found I didn't want to leave the church. I couldn't walk away. Perhaps part of me wanted to blaspheme more than anything.

Let Hell take me. Let my soul burn forever. Let me be disgraced in the eyes of men and God.

I knew what I wanted.

The only thing that remained for me to do was take it.

ONE

The monastery sat in a small village in Italy, a stone's throw from where I grew up. When I was a child, I was unruly. An unkept thief! Both my parents were alive in my youth, though my father was often away, and because we were a good Catholic family, my parents had seven children. All six of my siblings miraculously survived childhood, but nine mouths to feed proved unsustainable for my poor parents.

I liked to think of my exploits as holy in their own way, or at least, I came to think of them like this to avoid the shame of my thievery. By seven, I had been caught over a dozen times and beaten badly for at least half of those instances. But by ten, I had learned the skills necessary to lockpick, to move silently, to take only what wouldn't be noticed right away. Most of the time, all I was stealing was food.

My parents said nothing about how I came about the extra —until the mayor came knocking with a priest in tow.

I didn't have much choice. They wanted to exile me. Or kill me.

I said, "Let me repent," and the mayor looked at me and replied, "You will be repenting for the rest of your life."

I remember being almost thrilled. Thieving distracted me from what my young body was doing or thinking. I could avoid the feelings that arose when I saw strong men hauling crates or working fields. I could pretend I wasn't affected by the beautiful sights of them.

But as that monk priest leaned down and blessed me, accepted me into his fold, I remember crying with joy. I felt for the first time that I had hope. With the abbey and its brethren at my back, I could be protected from the Devil's influence. I remember my mother crying, too. On her knees as if in worship, saying, "Thank you, thank you, thank you. This boy is touched by Satan. He resists, but I do not know for how long. . ."

It was the last I saw of them.

As a monk priest, I spent my youth travelling through the rocky terrain, remote village to remote village, serving God as best I could in the chapels built to house Him. Worship Him. My days were spent leading services and taking confessions, and my nights were spent reading the Bible, praying, confessing, and inevitably dreaming.

When I returned to my village, I was thirty. Six years ago.

By the point of my return, I had been moulded into the image of a good, celibate man. I prayed daily. I was charitable. I improved. But as each day passed, I learned more and more that nothing really was going to change me.

Do you know the horror of that realisation? To see the Devil reaching for you every night, to realise that you live for the moments Satan gifted me: dreams of men's lips, their kisses, their touches, their cocks. To wake in shame, sweat-covered, seed spilt on the sheets, and to leave my chamber with a false mantra ringing in my ears: *holy, holy, holy.*

I tried. For decades, I tried.

Inevitability came for me anyway.

I made the decision when, one night, I was on my knees and deep in prayer, rolling a rosary over my fingers, praying to have those desires flayed from me once and for all, and I heard a voice.

I had perked up, for God had never visited me before. I thought: now it all pays off. Now you have proven yourself. Years of resistance and self-flagellation have brought God to your very doorstep. Praise it all.

Except, of course, it wasn't. It was the Devil himself, tiptoeing around my skull.

He said, "You came here thinking it would change you. You came here *hoping* it would. Choral singing and stained glass and the fetor of clogging incense—you wanted it to cleanse your insides. Destroy the infection in you with sacred light. And instead, two decades of it has made you this: barely contained, feral, furious. What has God's love given you except shame? What has God ever done for you?"

I stood and shouted this great cry of fear that called one of my brethren to my door.

"Alessandro!" he had called. Flushing and horrified, I opened the door to him.

Oliviero stood there. Twenty, barely a man, and with the innocence of a child. He was all blond hair, lanky limbs, and angular features. The roundest part of him were his large doe eyes. More than once, I had thought of kissing him—and more than once, I had cursed myself for it.

He was perhaps one of the purest people I have ever met, and without a doubt, I could tell he had been touched by the Lord, made good by him. Proximity to him had always unnerved me. Something innate in me rejected him. Even as part of me wished to touch him, a larger part of me understood that this desire was a result of my resistance. Desire had become cloying—almost anybody could relieve it. Almost anything.

"What happened?" he asked. He grabbed my shoulders and squeezed, asking again, "Were you alright? A bad dream?"

"Yes," I lied, and then I tried to be as honest as I could be. "The Devil telling me things."

Oliviero's face grew pale and worried. His hands slackened on my shoulders, and he nodded thoughtfully, with all the true concern of someone too good to be around a man like me.

What would he do if he knew me? If he knew the kind of man I was?

Would God call upon him to smite me? To remove my corruption from our church?

"To think the Devil would attempt to corrupt *you*, of all our brothers," Oliviero had said with a true and genuine smile. My gut roiled. "My advice: remember Bishop Jonah. Remember his teachings. If you do this, then we will be fine."

'We', he had said, like it was his battle too. How beautiful a man for his kindness. But he had invoked the name of Bishop Jonah, the old bishop who had ordained me—who had made me frightened. Though he passed years ago, I felt haunted by him. I had been taught. I had been trained. I had been beaten by him.

Even he had been unable to unstitch the Devil's handiwork.

"I will," I had told Oliviero. The lie tasted bitter in my mouth. "I will."

I had closed the door and gone back to prayer, only to hear the Devil's laugh.

My sleep that night had given me little rest. I dreamed extensively. Something called to me and showed me what could be.

I couldn't describe it. I saw my life as if I had chosen

myself over God. I saw all the men I might have tasted, the cocks I could have had inside me, the passion and the lust and the happiness I would have achieved if I hadn't concerned myself with Hell.

With this vision came the knowledge that my eternal life wouldn't grant me peace either. I would forever be a preserved bit of celibacy, suspended forever, having been untouched. Only my own hands had ever given me a taste.

"Summon me," the voice had said. "Summon me. I will give you what you want. I will touch you, I will desire you, I will show you years' worth of missed pleasure in a single night."

I woke. I lay there. I touched myself alone.

What was my soul worth? I had thought about it for hours. What was it worth, all of this? What was the point of Heaven if it would be eternal suffering?

Not this bland Hell.

Two

The decision was made.

The monastery was very old. Part of it was built into the rock of the village itself as if it were a natural growth. It was there that the monastery housed tomes and scrolls and holy books, and in this extensive archive was another section. A dangerous section.

There were brothers with a high power and a larger reach than I possessed. Where my roles involved spreading the word and attending to parishes, these men were dedicated to finding and confiscating the kind of dark tomes that might call the Devil to our world. Witchcraft, sacrilegious summons, descriptions of demons and their desires— the tomes there were under extensive lock and key, contained by holy wards, and meant to be protected by our brotherhood.

I walked the halls with a torch in hand. The shadows flickered wildly, undulating and pulsing against the stone walls. All the warmth had been leeched from the stone, and each step made me shiver. I told myself it was just the cold because, at this point, I could still pretend that I wouldn't follow through. But each step was another promise to the Devil: *I am coming. I hear your call, and I will follow you.*

If God was calling for me, then I did not hear it. Thirty-five dreary years—thirty-five wasteful years! It shouldn't have mattered anymore. It didn't matter anymore. I ignored the anxiety sent by God to deter me and gave up all hope of redemption.

Let the Devil have me.

The archive was behind an arched double doorway made of beautiful dark oak. A fat silver padlock barred an easy entrance, but there was another door sequestered in a corridor to the left. This one had once had a lock, but time had weakened it. An extensive stack of papers pushed from inside the archive. I had to put the torch in the sconce and press, press, press my body weight against it until it gave way. There was a dull sound of collapse. The door opened and stopped abruptly when it hit the fallen stack lumped at the bottom, but it was far enough that I could squeeze in.

Torch in hand once more, I stepped into the archive.

It was a dry room filled with dust. Shelves upon shelves of books spanned the long room, and two reading rooms were set up at the end I had walked into. The doors were hidden from my position by the bookshelves, but I knew I would be in one of those rooms before long.

Anticipatory heat spread to my groin.

My God, I thought, *is that all it takes?*

I walked immediately to the right, squeezing my way through a corridor framed by two overstuffed shelves. My torch remained high above my head, blazing away from any stray papers. At the end of this stretch lay an old, repurposed writing desk, locked in the same manner as the front door. I found a sconce for the torch and got to work.

It felt odd to summon this old skill of mine. I had not lockpicked for a decade. The last time I had done so was because an old cupboard in a parish chapel had been locked a decade earlier, and the key was lost. I had lockpicked it to discover a set of silver candelabra; the village had rejoiced.

Now, I lockpicked not for God but for myself.

The thrill was a pleasure of its own. When the lock shuddered and gave way, opening to me with a full-bodied click, I saw stars. My heart was racing, and my mouth was in an impossible smile—I was doing something for myself. Perhaps, perhaps, I was caught and sent here for this very moment. Perhaps it had been the Devil all along. *Let the boy believe he can be good. Let us prove over years and years of his life that he can't be. Let us show the man the truth of this matter; let us show him why Lucifer fell from Heaven.*

I sat back on my haunches. Dull torchlight showed me the insides of this old case, like the bowels of something long dead. Many scrolls were stacked on top of one another.

I took a deep breath.

I knew who had called to me. Who else could it have been? If I had been projecting my lust and my desire—decades worth of it bubbling inside me—then who else but the Prince of Lechery would reach for me?

Asmodeus.

I reached inside the case and let not God but Lust drive my hand.

Despite my intention, I was still surprised when the first scroll I pulled free had ASMODEUS in distinct black lettering. Quivering, heart racing, heat near blinding, I stood before I opened it and headed with the torch to the adjacent sitting room. Inside, I turned and bolted the door and put the torch in the sconce. Then, I stood alone in the near-empty stone room and breathed slowly and steadily.

There was nothing there but a desk, chalk for the slates if we wished to take notes and loose papers. The other room had the tools necessary for illuminating manuscripts, but I'd need the chalk for what I intended.

I opened the scroll.

Dust and the scent of caramel spore in the air.

The writing was neat and steady, and the scroll was decorated dutifully. It had been written with a reverent hand, a gentle hand. Someone like me, whose lust was so vital and vibrant it pulsed in their veins.

I felt a kinship to the author, and then a mote of jealousy took root. I wanted this more than them. I wanted this more than anyone has ever wanted anything. Damn it all to Hell.

The scroll read in Latin:

> *Ut eum evoces, vere desiderio impleri necesse est.*
> *Delinea symbolum. Hausce sanguinem.*
> *Eadem manu quae sanguinem haustit, te*
> *tangere ut velis tangi.*

> In order to summon him, you must be filled with
> true desire for him. Draw the symbol. Draw
> blood. With the same hand that drew blood,
> touch yourself as you wish to be touched.

I shook as I took the chalk and bent as if in supplication to sketch out the pentagram on the floor. While squatting inside it, I took a letter opener and used it to cut open the palm of my right hand.

Stinging pain sent a thrill through my body in rapid

pulses. The blood was warm, and I winced when I flexed my hand, feeling as the skin stretched and pulled and widened the wound.

Then came the question: how did I want to be touched?

I moved the layers of my priestly garb aside, still too ashamed to strip fully—ashamed to commit to this act and ashamed if I was wrong. If I couldn't summon this creature, I didn't want to be nude when the realisation hit me, cock and body covered in smears of my own blood.

I lay the scroll out in front of me, where Asmodeus was depicted in graphite that had faded long ago. I saw horns, the lick of a tail. I saw a broad, well-defined chest ghosting over the old paper.

In order to summon him, you must be filled with true desire for him.

I closed my eyes and summoned the thought of him. I imagined hands twice the size of mine running along my thighs. I imagined them loping around my neck, squeezing, pulling me forward. I imagined the beast doing what it wanted to my body, and I was too weak to resist. That was what I wanted. That was how I wanted to be treated. I would not be swayed from my path now; God had been a detour, and pleasure was the only thing I wished to worship.

Desire and warmth flooded to the base of my cock, which twitched before I'd even touched it. The first stroke urged it to harden. The blood leaking from my wound coated the shaft and sucked sensually against it with every tug; I was flushed and fighting shame in favour of this. I desired my satisfaction, but it took everything in me to focus, to allow myself this.

Isn't this what you wanted? Isn't this the kind of filth you have craved your whole life?

I imagined the voice was not mine but Asmodeus'. I answered loudly, clearly, and out loud.

"Yes."

I spread my legs. The cold night air did nothing to quell the heat in my groin, and as I stroked and the wet noises of blood slicking against my cock echoed against the stone, something happened that shifted me and this act away from crude pleasure. My body and my mind crystallised to that singular focus; a building rhythm in my groin, hand cupped with pestilent desire, the blood and the body: I achieved a kind of mysticism. The forefront of my mind collapsed under the weight of my excitement. I was gone from myself, and the animal in me took over to thrust, to grind, to steal every bit of friction it could from my blood-slick palm.

The air rose around me as if the sides of a coffin were boxing me in. Asmodeus in my mind's eye. Asmodeus filling me up. The rapture of its insistent touch and the force of its pressure bearing down on me was something that I couldn't ignore. Something kissed me, though I could see nothing. This presence began to learn my body and acquainted itself with my lips and my teeth. A warm tongue filled up my mouth and flicked over my incisors. I moaned throatily. Something sharp tore at my lip—I screamed out as the wet metallic taste pooled under my tongue. I buckled. My body twitched, confused as the conflicting sensations sparked in my brain. The pain, the pleasure—claws teased my skin, which split open under the invisible press of a large hand.

I came.

Within seconds, my eyes rolled back, and my body convulsed in the throes of the little death—a blinding, endless bit of liminality. My bloodied hand trembled, and I listed forward, sprawling in the mess I had made. Half suspended on my spread hands, I stared, panting at the mix of blood, cum, and sweat that now decorated the pentagram's interior.

It was done. It was inevitable, now.

I braced myself for a demon.

THREE

"What have you done?"

The voice echoed in that lonely stone room and made me shiver. My head shot up.

It was Bishop Jonah's voice. I was sure of it.

Unbidden memories came to me—his beatings, his teachings, his frequent scolding. My fingers dug into the filth-covered stone, tense and insistent. I hoped I would find purchase there; I craved the feeling of being anchored.

But my mind was clouded by the orgasm, and as the pulsing aftershocks faded, the nonsense of my fears became apparent.

I was alone, and Bishop Jonah was long dead. The voice had been in my mind.

I thought again of how often the old man scolded me when I was new to the holy order. What I had heard must have been the voice of guilt, like a puckered wound refusing to heal. Either my own or God's last attempt to keep his child pure.

Only, if God truly intended to keep me pure, He should have made me feel guiltier. Instead, I'd had years—decades!—

to overcome the guilt and the shame. I never would have gotten this far if *guilt* was enough to stop me.

Splayed there with the old scroll spread on the ground and my cock spent and dripping, pleasure, and stinging pain throbbing around my body, I struggled to feel anything but animalistic joy. A strange and blissful shock.

I had really done it. I had done something forbidden in the eyes of God — hell, in the eyes of any decent man — and the consequence was beginning to rise now from the pentagram of chalk and blood I had drawn on the clear stone floor.

It came together in a knitting of nerves, osseous matter, tendon, muscle, skin; a tapestry of life made from the wet gore of my own hand. Droplets of my blood were sucked through the air to join with this unholy making.

The godly man in me screamed. I shifted inexplicably away from the growing creature, frightened in that primal way where the core of you starts to open like a yawning chasm, and every other part of you drops inside. I knew if I didn't get a handle on it, I would be lost to the fear. Imagining running and leaving the Prince of Lust alone in a monastery—whatever dark scenario would play out; I knew I would regret fleeing.

You wanted this, I kept telling myself. *You have been wanting this for years.*

For my whole life. Every waking breath. Every dream.

I scuttled back inside the pentagram and stood to my full height, and as the demon materialised, it seemed to mimic me. Pink, puffy lungs expanded with sudden breath and were rapidly covered by tendons and muscle and skin. At once, everything came together and rendered it physical.

Asmodeus stood five feet, six, seven, and as the mist surrounding it dissipated, I choked in surprise.

. . .

To say the body was strong would be too lacking. The muscles were prominent, as if carved from marble, with the same sturdy density one would expect from a statue. It stood naked with its back turned to me, and I risked assessing it. Or, more accurately, my eyes wandered, grazing down its rippled back, where ridges grew from its spine to the tight waist and lower. Each thigh was the width of a small tree trunk. As if sensing me for the first time, it turned rapidly, sending its tail out to lick at the marble, the sound echoing like the clanging of steel against steel. I would have named it a beast. I had almost expected a beast. I would have taken anything. Anything at all willing to touch me.

But this. . .

It looked nearly human, if distended and much larger. The demon's torso was pure muscle, skin taut and rippling over its sinews, and its skin was a tawny brown. The light from my torch was thrown over its face, which was handsome, eyes dark and watchful. Its skin glowed. Briefly, I was rendered silent: I saw a vision of Asmodeus' glory, the prince surrounded by rings of hellfire, the whole body illuminated in beautiful destruction.

Fear thrummed through me, and something else, something deeper in me that Bishop Jonah had tried to beat out of me. Standing there, watching this thing materialise and knowing I wasn't going to run, knowing instead I wanted to stay, I realised maybe Bishop Jonah had been right all along. There was something wrong with me. There was a terrible desire in me, and there had been all along. Maybe my entire life. And the other thing, the worst realisation of all: if this was a test from God, I was going to fail.

The demon met my eye.

Instinctively, I darted backwards, not quite out of the pentagram. Was it a game I was playing or genuine fear? I could not tell you. Resistance and willingness fought for my attention.

The demon turned to look at me. My shoes squealed as they slid over the stone.

"I asked you a question, Alessandro. What have you done?"

I watched the demon say the words in the stolen voice of Bishop Jonah, and I thought about laughing. The cruelty of that, the delicious blasphemy of it. All that emerged from my mouth was a desperate exhale.

The demon shifted its head to inspect me, and its voice morphed to a stranger tone, jolting, deeper, gruffer. "Are you ashamed?" it asks. "Embarrassed? What would they say, all your brethren, if they knew what you *really* wanted?"

Everything in me lit up. Warmth pooled in my belly and lower, and my heart beat madly. I still couldn't help but flinch away from it. It was the size, I think, or the look on its face. Its eyes were the deepest black I had ever seen, save for a small gleam I'd like to think was amusement, which sparkled in the corner of its iris as it took in my squirming. The demon—Asmodeus—laughed.

The room rumbled with the sound. Dust dislodged from the ceiling and rained over us. The very core of my body tightened with anxiety and want; a smirk appeared on its lips. It stepped forward. I stepped back. We moved in a perverse little dance for a moment as I fought my open human fear, trapped in frightened muteness as the demon matched my every step. It looked me up and down, and its eyes turned bright and hungry.

Growling, it spoke. "You have summoned me with desire. With the open wet gore of your own body, you have pleasured yourself. You have thought of me and manifested me, and I can see what you want. You've been wanting it for years.

Someone to open up your body. To take it. To make you take it. To hold you down as they ruin you."

I shuddered. I had never—not once—heard it said so openly. The confidence with which it spoke and the nerves it sparked in me made me nearly instantly hard.

Asmodeus noticed. It glanced down between my legs and chuckled. "I know," it said, "Poor little lamb. But I want you to say it."

It stalked forward. Each footfall rattled the building, shooting vibrations up through my feet. Its tail flicked out like an agitated cat, whipping back and forth as it approached, and it bent down to better meet my eye, the way one might a child.

It reached out. A pointed, dagger-like claw scraped beneath my chin as it tilted my head back. The skin popped, oozing blood instantly. More gently than I thought I deserved, Asmodeus took my chin between forefinger and thumb, claws pressing into my puckered skin, and tilted my jaw until my neck strained.

"Filthy, blasphemous priest," it growled. "What do you want?"

I exhaled. That sigh—it had a weight to it. I wanted to move without words or to have things done to me, partly because I felt inexperience hovering like a guillotine above my neck and partly because I wanted absolution. I wanted to touch it and be touched. I wanted it to fuck me, stretch me, gape me, to render every waking moment I spent in the worship of God worthless. *Make me an object. Make me yours. Compare me to something to be discarded, something useless at best, a body to be fucked. Make me forget everything but the feel of your cock.*

But the slut was still a chained animal at that point, and I found I could say anything. I couldn't understand what I was feeling. Hadn't I wanted this? I had risked everything.

My priesthood. My reputation. Now that the demon was

here, I was a stuttering, embarrassing mess. All my inhibitions rose up. I remember the death throes of my faith rearing up like a spooked horse, screaming in the void of my lust-flooded mine: *you are a priest, for God's sake!*

The thoughts I was entertaining—imagining this demon taking me and pinning me against a wall, massive hands wrapping around my waist—I knew I shouldn't want that. I was too embarrassed.

Asmodeus grabbed my chin again, harder. The claws strained so hard I cried out, hissing against pain. Warm blood dribbled from the puncture wounds.

"Please," I managed.

"Ah," the demon said, smiling cruelly. "The bitch speaks."

I gasped, hands coming up in a pathetic resistance. I pushed weakly against the demon's wrist, as wide as my own thigh, and before I could say anything more, it dropped its hand from my chin and slid down to my neck. The grip tightened. I took a feeble breath and kicked as it lifted me from the ground. Sweat, stars, cock straining—my body reacted with uncontainable glee, but I was frightened. *It means to kill me.*

Then, the breath was knocked out of me.

My back hit the wall, and I half collapsed as the grip around my neck suddenly released. Fresh air scrabbled down my bruised oesophagus, and I clawed at my neck, gently pressing at the indentations where massive fingers and claws had pressed.

Asmodeus regarded me with sadistic disgust. I couldn't parse the expression. It enjoyed my reaction—but I knew without it saying anything that it thought me pathetic.

Why was I so aroused by that?

The demon approached. I turned my head up to stare up at it from underneath my brow. With a cooing, sweet sound, it reached out to me with a hand almost the size of my head. I closed my eyes.

"Look at me."

That was a command. I knew it, knew there was no playful question in that tone. Once again, Asmodeus dragged its clawed finger against my jaw. I breathed in. The scent of the demon was richly vile, sweet, and enticing, and I let it enter my lungs, almost grateful to breathe in its presence. But I winced as the skin split once more, and part of the claw dug roughly into an earlier wound. I imagined how I looked: flushed, desperate, bleeding. With my chin balanced on the edge of the demon's claw, it lifted my head upwards. Tentatively, I opened my eyes.

Asmodeus loomed over me, its black void eyes reflecting my frightened expression back at me. Its other hand grazed over my right arm, fingers sensually sliding through the cut on my palm. I jolted, first from the pain and then the arousal that shocked my body. My cock was swelling to erection, but if Asmodeus noticed, it did not do me the goodwill of touching me. Instead, a wolfish grin split its warm lips open, exposing two sharp canines and a long, forked tongue. Gently, it raised my arm, and I let it, suspended in a fugue state of helpless eagerness as it yanked my arm above my head. I realised what it was doing belatedly: those lips, those teeth, that tongue—it bent its head towards the wound and, its eyes transfixed on my own, it licked at the bloody palm.

Then, it was more than licking. Or rather, there was a dedication to the act now. Asmodeus' gaze grew dark and heavy with desire, and I felt myself growing hot. When that forked tongue prodded at the wound, digging in until it hurt, a small moan escaped me.

My legs were quivering, cock twitching in my pants, and I couldn't look away. Deliciously inescapable, we stared at one another as Asmodeus licked slowly, methodically, taking the blood I used to summon it into its body like a holy sacrament.

"You want me here," Asmodeus said. It was teasing me but

with the kind of confident surety that told me I needn't have bothered answering. It could tell. My body betrayed me, shivering with pleasure and swelling to erection. I still gulped, trying and failing to find some dignity to hold on to. What was I going to do? Lie to the demon? Send it back to Hell? Did I even want that—*no, you desecrator. You blasphemer, you slut. You want this. You want this!*

Everything I had done that night had been in a haze of lust. And the demon knew it. With one hand, it reached out to my clerical collar. All it needed was one sharp claw. Just like that, it sliced through the white collar, tearing it from my neck and throwing it to the ground.

My eyes flew wide. Naked, suddenly—or exposed in God's house. I opened my mouth, voice coming out in a cry of protest, but Asmodeus grabbed my face, slicing new wounds into the meat of my cheeks.

"If you're going to be my bitch," it growled, "you won't be wearing God's dog collar."

I whimpered like a proper dog and grew soft and pliable in the grip of a demon. Asmodeus leaned close. I could smell it. All-encompassing and intoxicating: sulphur, cedar, something strangely sweet like caramel — I couldn't help but lean forward into its strong body until it was supporting the weight of my traitorous body by my neck. It brought its lips to my ear, sharp teeth grazing against my earlobe, and move along my neck. That forked tongue licked over my lips with strangely sweet affection.

"Tell me what you want."

It spoke slowly and clearly, like I was stupid and needed to be told exactly what to do. And I did. I wanted the demon to order me around. I wanted to be absolved of free will, of misusing my free will for *this*.

"I—don't know."

I thought about Bishop Jonah as the demon breathed

heavily over me and imagined the way he used to ask me that same question.

A lot of lost lambs come to us. God points them in their holy directions. But you, Alessandro...

I was never so easy. Never so simple. But I tried.

On his deathbed, he had still called me that. Even after I had become a don. Alessandro, without the title. Tutted when I told him, "This. I want this. The monastery is my life."

"Don't you lie," he had said in between wheezing coughs. "It's a sin to lie."

And now, I had lied again. I told Asmodeus, "I don't know," despite my cock swelling. Despite baring my neck— free of God's mark, free of my priestly collar—to a demon. Despite loving it.

Even to my own ears, my voice sounded weak and pitiful. Asmodeus frowned, genuine and utter disappointment twinging across its face. It dropped the hold it had around my neck, stepped back—and slapped me.

Blood spurted from some part of me. I didn't know where— couldn't pinpoint the part of my face that hurt the most. My cheek was stinging from the impact and the puncture wounds. My lip burned with sudden ferocity. I spat blood out and coughed, and my hand shook as I reached up to touch the cut on my lip.

I looked back at the demon over my shoulder. It slouched, watching my expression carefully, curiously, poised as if expecting me to cry. Honestly, I don't know what I was feeling. All the anxiety had been struck out of me. I suddenly couldn't feel all the niggling thoughts of concern. I stood to my full height and turned to face it.

"Asmodeus," I said. "What are you going to do to me?"

The demon's expression ruptured like rot bubbling to the surface. That fine, handsome face imploded. Ridges, lines, fury, the smell of sulphur—it all increased tenfold. Asmodeus stalked forward and shoved me back. My back slammed hard against the wall, and I coughed as air struggled out of my lungs before I choked. One of those impossibly large hands had closed around me. Everything was cut off. Pain and a dull fog began in my head and my neck.

Asmodeus lifted me by my neck.

I kicked weakly, barely struggling. All the blood pooled into my cock, abandoning my head. I quickly grew light-headed. The world fogged and blurred. I couldn't breathe. A glimpse of its true nature, I thought. A revelation.

The demon leaned forward. Its breath, half vile and half sweet, loped into my open mouth and coated the roof.

"You don't call me that name," it told me. Ordered me. "You are an ant to me. A toy. An object to be used."

"No," I wheezed, nodding feebly. "No, of course not. I'm sorry."

The demon's grip tightened. "Address me by my title. Prince of Lust. That is my name to you, slut. "

I started babbling, gasping air as my voice cracked. "Yes, yes. Prince of Lust. My Prince..."

"Good boy," the prince said. Without further ceremony or questioning, it threw me roughly to the side. I hit stone and started to crawl away on instinct, exposed and panting hard. I will admit a bit of ego seeped into me then because I thought, *what am I doing? What am I doing?*

I was full of fear. I had summoned something dangerous, lustful, ravenous. I knew innately it would not leave before it had come for what I had called it to do.

I couldn't pretend I wasn't eager. Neither did I want to pretend. Besides, there was no point. Both myself and the demon knew what I wanted. I saw the prince staring at me, low knowing look glinting in those dark eyes.

All I had to do was surrender. Be the slut I had always

known myself to be. Forget everything I had been taught about being chaste and good and boring. I was sick of it.

My vestments were torn. A button lay outside the pentagram circle, ripped away from my chest. Would it tear the rest of my clothes off me, I wondered? Did I want it to?

I looked back over my shoulder and ,teasingly, I began to spread my legs.

The prince chuckled. The sound made my heart race. *Pathetic*—I heard that somewhere deep in my skull, but I don't know whose voice it was. Bishop Jonah, or my own squirming morality. I don't know whether the Prince of Lust himself had said it because the way it looked at me was scathing.

The demon stepped forward and wrenched my head back by my hair. Blood drizzled from my scalp where its claws scratched me. A few sapless sounds edged out from my lips; I arched towards the force of its hand.

Once again, it asked me, "What do you want?"

I knew what to say this time. I bit my lip and rolled my eyes as far back into my skull as I could, hoping to see the prince's eyes. Like that, straining and shaking, I spoke.

"You."

The demon smiled. "Good."

FOUR

I t did not wait.

I realised later that it could have taken me at any point. That everything until now was a curious game of consent—or perhaps something baser, like a play at humiliation. There was a vulnerability in asking for it, begging for it. The first time I had ever spoken the truth so willingly.

I knew immediately it would want me like that again. Pathetic and begging and praying until I was invoking it the way I would God.

The prince dropped my head and moved its hands to my waist. I sighed, eyes rolling closed. Those hands wrapped all the way around me, fingers nearly able to lace together. But it slowly pressed its claws into my abdomen, pressing so firmly the organs began to bulge around the demon's fingers.

It will gut you, I thought. Bishop Jonah thought. *It will gut you. It will fuck your insides. It will leave you to die.*

I imagined briefly what that would be like. The vivisection, belly torn open, and organs exposed and steaming. I imagined pain giving way to a perverse pleasure, a cock slipping over the looping heat of my intestines, and I found myself wondering if it would keep my vessel holy. If this kind of dese-cration, where my ass remained unfucked, and my cock untouched, would still allow me to take God's love and hold it firmly in my hands.

Heaven won't touch you. Not when you want this so badly.

The prince could do whatever it wanted to me. I was help-less to stop it—a thrilling thought. I was prey, then; my mind slipped towards that instinct. With my heart thundering and my back growing slick with panicked sweat, I let my mind fall towards prey instinct.

The demon let go of my waist and dragged its hooked nails over my back. Fabric ripped as the vestments were shredded, and the skin beneath it flayed back, too. I startled forward with a hiss and was quickly yanked back into position.

"Stay still," it told me. I stayed still.

One warm, roughly calloused hand pressed into the small of my back. The force pushed me down until both legs spread open. My hips strained with the angle, but I didn't dare resist. I squeezed my eyes shut. The prince took the other hand and struck it across my ass.

It was not a kind strike. I remember howling—an embar-rassing, ragged sound. Keeling forward through the shout, I rectified my position quickly, and the prince clicked its tongue. Two fingers ghosted across the sting, easing my shaking body. A strange kindness.

I wanted to know what it thought of me. Was I obviously eager? Willing? What would it do to make me into a begging slut?

You would beg for it right now. Nothing would need to be done to you.

God, I am sorry, but it was true. I would have begged. Pleaded. Instinctively, I arched my back for it. A heavy warmth grew from the base of my balls, and the throbbing heat of my cock was close to overwhelming. The seam of the vestments grazed against the sensitive head. The friction stung, almost, and yet I was grinding forward against the pressure of my own clothes.

The prince's fingers glided over the tenting bulge in my pants. I exhaled harshly, rutting towards the fleeting pressure. *Touch me*, I thought. *Touch me.* I wanted to be crushed by it. I wanted more—more—immediately.

I arched with a muffled whine, shuddering, close to tears. Far harsher than I meant to, I screamed, "Just tear them off me! A—ah!"

My neck crunched as it was pulled back. Another fistful of my hair, another disappointed growl. I had to push myself up onto my forearms and lean back to stop the hair from being pulled from my scalp.

The demon cupped my left hip and leaned close to my ear again. That forked tongue flitted out, sucking at my ear lobe. "Shut the fuck up, you stupid slut."

It shoved me down by the neck before I could say anything more. My cheek met the stone with a scrape, and I wriggled uselessly until I could get my hips up again. I arched. I said nothing else, not even an apology.

The demon said, "Good."

I couldn't say what I wanted, but at this point, my mind had grown fuzzy with a deep and desperate urge. I was supposed to be waiting for instructions. Doing what I was told. But the thought of prayer came to me. Filled me up with a purpose. Desperation and frustration came together and dulled my senses until I almost asked for divine intervention. *God, I come to you as your pathetic child. Please have this demon touch me. Please let it fill me. Fuck me. Use me. Use me. Use me.*

It reached around again, the monstrous hand brushing against the bulge in my pants. I moaned and thrust into it, but the demon's grip on my left hip stopped the movement. I groaned in protest. I broke the rules.

"Please," I moaned. The word took an entire breath to say, coated in a lustful ecstasy.

"Ah, ah," it said. "You eager thing. Be patient. I want to see you squirm."

I took a deep breath, the way I might before a service. I had wanted this for years. Far too long. But I wasn't about to jeopardise this chance by being an overeager slut. I could be obedient. The life of a priest is true obedience.

I swallowed and waited for the demon. It moved painfully slowly. I heard the quiet laughter in its breath and knew I was being played with.

It's laughing at you. Your wretchedness. Your eagerness. Look at you, splayed and wanting, legs spread to be fucked.

I gritted my teeth and stayed still, waiting. In one smooth motion, its fingers popped open the top button on my pants. Ever so slowly, it moved to the next one.

"Is this what you've wanted?" it asked. I could hear the smile in its voice. "Is this what you've lusted for? Dreamed of? Have you thought of this and touched yourself? Climaxed to it?"

I moaned at every question. The metallic taste of blood bloomed in my mouth, and I shuddered towards each slight touch the prince offered me.

"Tell me," it said. "Have you fucked your own fingers before?"

I gasped. Shuddering, desperate, and eager, I told it, "Yes."

But the moment shuddered to a stop, ruined, interrupted.

Someone screamed behind me.

FIVE

I went still, breath caught in my throat. Blood rushed to my face. If I had thought I'd escaped shame, it all came back to me tenfold and with a vengeance. I felt the demon move. All the pressure from my waist vanished as it stood, and hot air rushed into my half-crushed lungs. Without its support or its control over my body, I collapsed against the stone, shivering. Shock and latent arousal made me slow. I should have been up by now, saving face, defending myself or. . .

Or what? Will you let this demon ravage the monastery? Will you let it fuck someone else?

I had no right to be jealous, and yet I felt that keen sense of possessiveness drawing me tight, a thread pulling through my centre towards the demon's body.

The Prince of Lust growled low and angry, a deep rumble in its throat that descended into a hideous roar. It paced agitatedly as Oliviero screamed.

I gathered myself, stuffing my half-hard cock into my undergarments and pulling the remains of the shredded vestments around myself. But after that, I sat there like a fool. Fear and shame made my mouth run dry.

I didn't know what to do. I had been caught. In the vein of a damned man, I saw the entirety of my life flash in my mind's eye: a second of time, a blip on this earth. Every squandered opportunity, every moment I had denied myself. The power I'd allowed Bishop Jonah to have over me. The power he still had, even after his death.

Anxious rattling in my mind, a voice saying, *If they work out what you've done. . . If they knew how much you wanted this* —no. In the seconds it took Oliviero to scream, I saw all of this, then crawled forward until I found the strength to stand.

Oliviero—beautiful, blond, *young* and innocent—stood slack-jawed and terrified. He was barely a man, just blond curls, sad chin hairs that sprouted intermittently; innocent shock. Seeing him spurned cruelty to swim into my mind. Rage, too. He had interrupted. He was standing and sputtering, pointing at something ancient and beyond him. I surprised myself with a shocking amount of anger. I thought about killing him. Wringing his neck. Punishing him. I thought about taking my lust out on his body in the form of its brother: rage, anger, fury —had I always been like that? Was it the sulphur and the proximity to the demonic creature that was corrupting every moral thing in me? Or had it always been there?

Your mother saw it. Saw you. *She knew before the others what you really were. Are. What you hope to become. What you want done to you.*

No. *No.* I didn't want harm to come to Oliviero. Not really. This interruption was just bad luck.

I started to say, "Olivi—"

My voice drowned beneath another one of his boyish screams. The demon moved forward, clawed hand swiping at the air.

Oliviero's eyes shifted to the pentagram on the floor. Colour drained from his face.

I knew what he was going to do. I couldn't stop it.

"No!"

I pushed forward with my shout. All the work I had done, how long I'd waited, everything I'd risked drawing that perfect symbol—the thought of what I would lose eclipsed all this fear. My eyes shifted to Asmodeus. But the boy thought he was saving me.

He rushed forward and skidded across the floor, destroying the clean, solid lines of the pentagram. Panting, he looked up with a smile, expecting the demon to have dissipated.

Nothing happened.

My heart seized. It felt like a reunion or a homecoming: that quiet relief at finding something lost again, at accessing something real within nostalgia. Not a hair was out of place on the demon's perfect body. Its breathing was erratic and quick, and its fingers twitched in uncontrolled spasms by its side, but it was *still there*.

Seeming to realise this itself, Asmodeus roared triumphantly and pounded across the floor. I stood terrified. Felt childlike. I saw it all play out. The demon's claws would cut across Oliviero's throat. He would choke on the blood or, if the prince pressed hard enough, would be decapitated with a strike. Arterial blood would spray, and the body would crumble, and then what? A boy dead and me alone again—I didn't want to think about it anymore. I worried about myself and the kind of person I might become in that interim moment, the liminal space and time where I could let myself be fucked by a demon in the blood of a brother before I had to decide what to do with myself. Would I tell the truth? Continue living as a don? Regret what happened to the boy so I could be stretched and gaped and filled?

"Stop!"

I shouted so desperately my ragged voice cracked under the strain. Asmodeus shuddered to a halt. I heard its body stop, like a carriage halting suddenly, iron creaking, clanging, groaning. It turned slowly to stare at me. I cannot describe the look in its eyes. The disgust, the rejection, the utter disdain. This being was older than anything I could've comprehended, and I was made worthless in its gaze. I dropped to my knees. The way I might in worship, I said, "Mercy. Have mercy."

God, have mercy on me, a sinner. Luke 18:13. It became a mantra in that long stretch of a second.

"Ant," Asmodeus rumbled. "A pestilence, your kind." Its tail lashed out at me, and that sharpened end dragged slowly across my jaw. "Tell me what to do again, and I will dance in your blood."

But before it could threaten me—or tease me—further, Asmodeus vanished into smoke.

The loss I felt was sinister and dark. I frowned in puzzlement and then despair, not understanding the full sense of emptiness that had opened in my guts. I must have looked shocked or otherwise pathetic because Oliviero scrabbled up to me. I turned away from him. My cock had started to grow soft, shocked into flaccidity, but I still tried to hide it from the boy. The thought kept coming: *don't let him see how aroused you were. Don't let him know how much of a slut you really are.*

Oblivious, Oliviero was mumbling a prayer, hands moving instinctively in the sign of the cross and blessing me in the same way. I did not feel blessed. I felt trapped.

"Don Alessandro," he murmured. I thought he might hold me or touch me; he kept leaning close as if desiring an embrace. "Are you okay?"

I didn't know what to say. I gave him a small smile and nod.

He searched my face, frowning. "How did this happen?"

I shook my head. Silence would be my friend: I had no other excuse.

I stumbled here and found it like this—weak.

I ended up gesturing to the room and said, "I heard a noise. Growling," and then I trailed off, hoping shock was a good enough cover for my lack of detail.

"If I hadn't come," Oliviero began and then flushed. "I do not mean to claim I've saved your life, don, but. . ."

It was exactly what he meant, but I couldn't fault him. Ego and youth go hand in hand, even amongst the faithful. I reached out and squeezed the man's shoulder. But his eyes had wandered. He spotted the scroll I used to summon Asmodeus and another burr caught in his brow.

"That is meant to be under lock and key."

I stood slowly and approached it, feigning surprise. I glanced at him and tried to strike some conspiratorial bond between us without a word. Oliviero looked frightened. It was a delicious expression, all twisted brows and short, staccato breaths.

"I'll take the book to the restricted section," I said, like all of this was nothing. I don't know—I couldn't bring myself to act scared. I hoped shock would be a good excuse for my despondence. As I picked up the scroll, I caught a glance of the sketch—of Asmodeus' hulking body. I pressed it close to my chest.

Oliviero stands too. "We must contact the bishop," he said. "Tomorrow, anyway. You should sleep; I can take it back for you."

"No," I said it too quickly. Oliviero flinched. I summoned some kind of lie and tried to soften the blow. "I don't want to put you in any danger, Oliviero, and this book... is about as dangerous as you can get."

His eyes went wide with the kind of trusting innocence that a child would have for its parent. The guilt struck me hard, but I had committed to the act now, you see. Return was not possible, nor was it wanted.

But Oliviero accepted my words. He blushed and nodded, then slipped out of the room, all legs and awkward height. He flashed me one final look before he disappeared for good, and as soon as he was out of sight, I forgot about him completely.

After coming so close, after being so hard and so willing to let Asmodeus, Prince of Lust, have its way with me, there really was no going back. God's collar lay abandoned on the floor. I did not kneel to pick it up.

I wasn't God's anymore. Perhaps I had never been.

No matter what it took, I made the covenant there with myself. No matter the ritual, the sacrifice, the blasphemy, the price, I was going to be that demon's toy.

Six

I tossed and turned for hours.

I'd tucked the tome under my pillow for safekeeping. Or perhaps because I wanted to be close to the demon, or I hoped that closeness to it might award my body somehow. It felt stupid admitting that; the Prince of Lust would not return unless I summoned it.

I slept fitfully. I kept waking up in an intense sweat, sheets slick, and my body shaking. Each time I was rock hard, cock desperate, pulsing under the sheet. The first two times I woke up, I took my cock and worked myself until I came, thinking of the demon's cock inside me, its grip around my waist, how it could use me like a cock sleeve—use me however it wished. I imagined the way I would be twitching and gaping at the end of it, cum leaking from me. Had, used, and discarded. By the third time I awoke, horny and desperate, I gave up. Relief wouldn't come; I had been using my hands for decades, and it wasn't enough. It had never been enough, and now I that had seen what could have been, it would do nothing for me. Instead of touching myself a third time, I sighed and turned over, trying to sleep.

Eventually, a deeper sleep came. I had an hour or two of uninterrupted rest before the dreams.

At first, they were vague. I only saw shapes and some colours, skin mostly, the demon's hands flashing into view. Nothing really happened in those dreams except impressions of taste and smell and touch, and they flowed through me easily. Then detail snaked into them; the scent of the prince, its fragrant cedar and caramel, with the smell of my own sweat and cum mixed with it. I watched the demon materialise again, growing out of ash and blood like it had when I first summoned it, only now it lunged at me the instant it materialised. It saw me, and its cock hardened and blushed a dark red at the tip; the shaft was thick with bumps plumping to firm ridges as it grew erect. I let it grab me by the neck again, lift me, and throw me against the wall, raking my skin red and raw with its claws.

There was nothing coherent to what happened next, no reality to it. But it felt good to dream. I was pushed against the wall. My legs were spread. I arched down into position with decades worth of eagerness, and the prince's cock split me apart, slipped inside like I was made for it, ridged and tugging on the warm wetness of my insides. I had nothing of that size to compare it to—it had only ever been my fingers—but my mind translated it as a fullness. A satiation that seemed heavenly and impossible after so much dripping lust.

The demon didn't even have to thrust to have me close to the edge; I generated enough friction on my own, squirming and grinding back with unstoppered desire. And I *couldn't* stop myself, not even when I had the vague awareness this was just a dream. I squeezed my ass and felt the answering pulse of the cock inside me. Asmodeus growled and rammed up into me, and I screamed freely, eagerly, head thrown back as it crowded me close to the wall, yanking my head back by a fistful of my hair. When it kissed me, it felt ravenous; the prince made a meal of me, hammering hard and without mercy, thrusting and pushing. As it came, it growled deep, and I felt the sticky warmth of it coat the inside of my ass. The cock popped free of my twitching hole, and I shuddered through my own orgasm, warm cum from my gaping ass dripping down my leg.

I felt like such a slut. Such a good little slut.

I woke with a start. I shot up in bed and realised I'd cum again and was now lying amongst my own mess. Shame pricked at my skin again, but the embers of desire helped burn it away. Like some sacred or holy blessing on me, like a ward against evil, each orgasm at the thought of that demon had muted those feelings.

By that point, it was probably four or five in the morning. Dawn would come some, and with it, a retribution I dreaded.

I hadn't interacted much with the new bishop. I knew he was an old, conservative man, but they all were. I had almost expected someone from our flock to be named abbot, but the church had sent another bishop to us—most likely for the evil we protected in the form of those tomes. Still, before he had even arrived, I'd decided not to know him. Bishop Jonah's ghost still haunted me and I didn't want to realise just how little I had grown by allowing myself to be, once again, influenced by another of these officials.

But the fear I had, the one that just nearly suppressed my lust that night, was that the bishop would be alerted, he would swoop in and efficiently remove every dangerous tome under the monastery's care, and then an inquisition would be held to find the culprit.

You see, I wasn't much worried about that last point. It felt almost inevitable that I would be found out, and I'd developed a kind of numbness around that. It was the thought of the tomes being ripped away from me. Any chance I had to contact Asmodeus, Prince of Lust, again being taken and

LUCIEN BURR

destroyed. The growing horror that if this demon did not fuck me, nobody would—or no average man would ever be enough.

Really, what was there to be ashamed of? If anything, holding back, pretending this wasn't what I wanted— surely there was more shame in that? If I could be honest with myself, honest in the eyes of God, then that was better than lying for the rest of my life. It felt more honourable. More blessed. And in all honestly, the dream I had only proved how insidious my desire was. Lust fired through my veins.

A dream was only a dream. But I wanted to feel the real thing.

I wanted the demon to pick me up and throw me around, to use me completely, to fuck every thought out of my head.

Render me nothing but yours. Make me your slut, your hole, your toy; I will be nothing else. Not Don Alessandro. Not a man. Not even that.

Stronger than any covenant God ever made, that feeling. Stronger than shame, too. I said it like a prayer: make me a ruin.

I needed Asmodeus. I needed it right then and there.

I threw the covers off and lit two lamps before I went to the door and bolted it.

The room glowed with light. It was like a small cell, all cold stone. The bed—simple by design—took up most of the room, and the only other piece of furniture was a modest bedside table that housed an equally unremarkable oil lamp. I sat down on the edge of the bed and looked down at my hands. The palm had been bandaged, but the wound still wept. Pink oozed through the cotton. Gingerly, I removed the bandage and exposed the puckered flesh beneath. It hadn't been long enough to heal, and in fact, Asmodeus' forked tongue had pried the cut open even deeper than I had first made it.

What if it made it larger? What if it used that wound to pleasure itself? Made it stigmata, made you holy with every thrust until you were stretched in the form of crucifixion, until you could look at your reflection in its black eyes and see the Son of God looking back?

Desire felt complicated.

I ignored the aching throb of my spent cock and turned to the pillow where I'd tucked the scroll away. I pulled it out, and locked eyes instantly with the sketch of the demon.

I made a low noise. Pathetic. *Pathetic*—I heard that rebound through my skull in Bishop Jonah's voice and then in the prince's. The effect was another aching throb through my appendage. I didn't have to do much to coax it to attention.

Whilst I still had some control over my sanity, I stood and drew the pentagram in chalk around my bed. I'd slept in nothing, and so, already naked, I lowered myself onto the bed.

I had no knife with me, but I had teeth. I closed my eyes and summoned the demon in my mind. Asmodeus' forked tongue flicked against the weeping wound. I tasted myself in a new way, shivering at the odd sweetness and the metallic undercurrent. Then, I bore my teeth and pressed the sharp edge of my canine against my palm.

Very simply, it hurt. I squeezed my cock for the slight shuddering pleasure it offered me, and my mind split. The stupid, cum-hungry slut roared to life and started a chorus of quiet, eager moaning. *Yes, yes, yes*—I gnawed at my palm, and that part of me revelled, knowing that when I bled, when I touched myself, when I thought of it, Asmodeus would come to me. The other part of my brain was the base, fearful primitive. Pain shocked it to life, and it reared up with a scream. *What are you doing? You're hurting yourself—stop it. Stop it.*

I did not stop it.

Not until I tasted blood.

That time, instead of working my cock, I dipped my

fingers in the oil from the lamp and edged those warm, blood-slicked fingers to my own ass.

I pressed in.

There's always a moment at the beginning where one's body tries to reject the interloper. It happened to me then—a pushing sensation, a bodily refusal, but I didn't stop. I put another finger inside, scraping it over my own prostate, shivering at the jolt of feeling. I fucked myself.. I degraded myself for the act of it—I was a slut. By sunrise, every priest in the place would know what kind of sick man I was. By that point, it wouldn't matter. I'd belong to the demon, not to God.

I bounced on my own fingers and called its title aloud. *Prince of Lust, Prince of Lust.* I touched myself sparingly, like the sacrament—this orgasm would be given to me by the prince itself and not my own mortal hand. I thought about the filthy things I wanted it to do to me—the things I might have let it do if it wanted to, if it asked me. The complete and utter surrender I would offer it, even when partaking, would send me straight to hell. I'd held it at bay for years, but now there was no stopping it. One taste of my fantasy, and it was all I could think about.

Please, I prayed, *please, please, please, please.*

Sulphur. Cedar. A pleased, airy laugh.

"Virgin on a technicality alone," a deep voice said, amused. "You have desecrated yourself many a time. You desecrate yourself now."

"Yes," I said. I opened my eyes, and there it was: monstrous, hungry, watching. I slowed my movements and started to pull my slick fingers out of myself, but Asmodeus hissed. Its face crumpled into fury, and it rushed forward, slamming its fist against the wall to my left. I jumped and shuddered, sliding further down onto my fingers with a protracted groan. The force of its punch was so strong that brick indented around the large fist. Dust fell to the floor. I gulped and slowly met the demon's gaze.

"Never said stop," it hissed.

I moved slowly, doing as I was told. I started bouncing, and it tutted me. That liquid-quick tail lashed forward and sharply edged beneath my chin. The skin seared as the pointed tip carved a cut through the soft flesh. I winced, clenching involuntarily around my own cramping hand.

"Slowly, boy," it whispered. "Show me how much you want it."

So, I showed it. A natural nervousness washed over me at first, and I had to close my eyes to move with such intentional slowness. But the demon made a pleased noise, and it opened something in my gut. Another one of lust's cousins: compliance. Submissiveness. Obedience. It dawned inside me the way desire did, growing steadily hot until I was in a haze. I drooped forward and spread my legs, angled so the demon could watch.

And it *was* watching. Very intently. My cock was twitching, the pink head swollen and dripping precum down onto my twisted thigh. The demon approached and I watched it from underneath my lashes, panting shakily as one of its fingers glided up my thigh. The claw scraped at the skin, but then it pressed the round rise of its finger over the pooling precum and put it to its lips.

"You summoned me again," it said with something akin to wonderment. "You must really be desperate."

"Yes," I told it. "Yes."

"Say it."

"I'm desperate."

"For what?"

"For cock. For *your* cock." I mindlessly rode myself faster and started babbling. "I want you. I want you to scrape my insides. Fuck me. Use me. Make me your slut."

It grabbed my face and squished my stinging cheeks. "You

already are my slut," the prince said. I glanced down at its cock, which was swelling now. The ridges rose slowly until it bumped in a beautiful way. My mouth opened.

Asmodeus moved one large hand to the back of my head. Its palm encompassed me, warm fingers pressing on either side of my cheek. "Pathetic little whore," it murmured, pulling my whole body towards it. My fingers popped out of my hole, and I splayed both hands on the bed. My head was hot and empty and wanting. Asmodeus smiled at me, handsome face twisting up with sadistic glee. Then it gripped my hair so tightly I screamed. It shook me. Happy at how limp I was, the demon laughed, and shoved my mouth down onto its red, twinging cock.

My screaming moan was muffled and then choked to death in my throat. The prince was neither kind nor slow with me; it rammed into my mouth. The girth ached my jaw, and I felt the tip slide over the opening of my throat. The ringlike muscle caught it, and Asmodeus forced itself deeper. Barely half of it could fit. I gagged. Thick, stringy saliva pooled out of my mouth around it.

"Such a fucking slut. Listen to you," it hissed. "No godly man would love this. No good man would want it. Tell me."

It dragged me off its cock by my hair. Saliva dripped onto the sheets. I coughed and spluttered, and the prince shook my head like a doll.

"Hm?" it prompted. "Say it."

Rasping, I said, "I love it. I love it."

I wished I could've taken it all. For a moment, Asmodeus' grip on my hair slackened, and it let me do as I pleased—and pleasing it is what pleased me. I laid the head of its cock beneath my tongue like holy communion and let the precum seep there. I took it into my body spiritually, and I felt it. I felt then what my brethren had claimed to feel all along. God's voice in their ears, God's light, God's love. I had this. I had

Asmodeus, Prince of Lust. I had the ecstasy of sex and I worshipped it gladly.

The demon let me suck and lick and moan, and when it wanted more, it grabbed my hair again and shoved itself deeper into my throat. I gagged and spluttered and splayed my hands against its stomach, pushing weakly and half-committedly against the firm muscle. Then I gave in; I slacked and relaxed and did my best to be a good slut. I let it have its way with me, and my moans became infrequent and reactive as my eyes rolled back into my head. I left my body. I felt warm.

"I could do whatever I want to you, couldn't I?" it murmured. "My sweet little priest."

I was barely conscious of its words, but heat rushed to my groin again. I loved the way it spoke to me. I love how it could see how desperate I was.

"Fuck me," I begged. "Please. Please, my prince, please, fuck me."

I knew I was a mess at this point. Sweat smeared my hair to my forehead, and my mouth was covered with thick, ropey saliva. I was near bowing before this demon. But I wanted it. A near pain spasmed through my cock, and I rutted pathetically against the bed for the friction it offered me.

The demon laughed at me. "Pitiful whore." Its hand slammed down over my neck and I collapsed into the pillow with a high cry. It moved a finger down to the left of my ass, claw dragging slowly over the sensitive skin.

"Wait," I said automatically. I squirmed but it just held me down with more pressure. "Wait, wait, your claws—"

"Shh," it hushed me and pressed inside.

I whimpered, first from the bright and sharp pain and then the feeling of it dragging in and out of me. The demon moved slowly, and I'd already opened myself on my own fingers. This wasn't about preparation. It was about the pain. The process. It added another, and then another, and worked me like that. I loudly moaned into the pillow, trying to keep my body relaxed. When it grew bored of this, it pulled its fingers free. I clenched on instinct and it laughed.

"Only a whore's body would react like this," it told me. Its big hand slapped down on my back several times. Its voice sounded warm and pleased. I grunted with every slap of its hand, the force thundering through my chest. "Masquerading as a priest all these years. I can't think of a greater sin. Not when your hole is *hungry*."

Two warm hands clamped down on my hips and shifted me, dragging me back onto my knees. I braced myself and closed my eyes. It was happening. Finally, finally—and then I howled.

Whatever entered me was not the firm, round girth of a cock. There was a sharp sting and a thin, rope-like wiggling pulsing in and out of my body. Every jutting stroke glided over my prostate, and my body fell helpless. My eyes rolled to the back of my head, I drooled with an overwhelmed pleasure, and I let myself be fucked like that.

"Oh, look at you," Asmodeus said. "Helpless. Shameful. Defenceless." Its fingers darted playfully across my back. I moaned when it picked up the pace, tail whipping into me. I squirmed around, my body arching off the bed. The prince pulled my head back. "Little priest, you are the most willing piece of meat I've ever fucked."

God. *God.* I couldn't even pretend the demon was wrong. Every thrust had me jolting.

I realised belatedly the thing fucking my insides roughly was its tail. It pressed further inside, and that sharp tip knicks something soft and sensitive—I rolled forward with a strangled scream, and the tail slid quickly out of me.

With one strong, fluid motion, Asmodeus flipped me. It pinned both my hands above my head, crushing against my wrists. My legs were levered apart, but when it bucked at me, I raised my legs obediently until it had folded me into an exposing press.

I still had the awareness to flush.

"I think we're beyond embarrassment now." Asmodeus' tongue licked out, sucking at my earlobe. Warm breath tickled at my neck; every exhale laced with a deep-throated growl. I knew it wanted me, which made me rut against nothing but the cold night air. The pressure left my wrists, and it pressed down onto my chest, moving its head to lick at my underarms, to raze its teeth across my chest, to suck and bite at my nipples. My cock trembled, and Asmodeus didn't touch it once. Not once.

"*Please*," I whined. My hole twitched. The urge to be filled was one that grew from the core of my belly and pulled like gravity. I'd take anything. I'd take its tail again. Its clawed fingers or my own hand.

But, dear God, I wanted its cock.

Asmodeus reared back and scraped its hands down my naked chest. Red welts rose immediately and it smiled, broad and happy at the sight. When its cock slapped against my belly, I froze. My whole body reacted the way I might before an angel. I felt frightened by its age; felt the edges of my own mortality.

Gently, teasingly, it rubbed itself against the down of hair on my stomach, catching the side of my own cock every few strokes.

I dropped my head back into the pillow and groaned, frustrated. Please. Please. I'm breaking—can't it tell? Can't it tell?

"I'll do anything," I whispered, and I meant it. "I'll do anything, just *please*."

It raised one pointed brow. "I believe you, slut," it whispered, almost sweetly. "Such keenness in your face. And your body. . ." A finger pressed to the throbbing tip of my cock.

"*Fuck*."

The prince chuckled and glided its fingers up my chest with awful, playful slowness. Then it pushed the pad of its finger into my jugular and leaned forward with a hungry, malignant gleam in its eyes.

Its dark eyes encompassed me. "Are you God's bitch?"

I stared at it. I felt compelled to keep my mouth shut. A snarl crossed the demon's face, and it pressed closer to me, folding my legs even further so my feet bobbed in my periphery. It slid its cock against me and pressed against my hole—pointedly, not enough to push inside, but enough for my body to react. Frustration and something more sinister—the same kind of violence that filled me when Oliviero interrupted us—entered me now.

"Fuck me," I told it.

It slapped me. Hard. My head sprung to one side. Pain blistered across my cheek, but when I opened my mouth, I was smiling. Self-flagellation is not new to me, and this? This felt not like religious discipline but ecstasy.

"I said." The Prince of Lust growled and whispered against my ear. "Are you God's bitch?"

I shivered and felt its cock throbbing against me. I was inches away from losing my mind to this beast, seconds from irrevocably changing my life and letting myself be free and wild and filled.

I glanced up at it. I made sure it was seeing me—and seeing me truly. It tore God's collar from my throat, and I didn't pick it up. I risked title and station and honour, my very life, my mortal soul, to summon it into existence. I haven't been God's for a while.

"No," I told it. "I'm yours."

It grinned. Then, both giant hands pressed against my inner hips and pushed my legs apart as far as they would go.

My breathing went erratic, eager, wanting. My groan was

low and long as the demon's cock slowly slid inside. I tensed around it, and then I howled.

There's nothing else for a moment. My body was hot and full—full to bursting. I kept clenching and unclenching instinctively around the thing twitching inside me. Asmodeus rolled its hips and ignored whatever high-pitched whines I was making.

"Wait," I murmur, "wait, I can't—"

It slowed, dragging itself all the way out so I could feel my hole twitching and pulsing around nothing but the air. Then it plunged back into me. I screamed and snapped back against the sheets, fingers twisting desperately for purchase.

And then it started slamming me.

I nearly passed out. I was breathing short, shallow breaths. The air struggled into my lungs and was half of it expelled with every brief, reactive moan. I slid into a different state. The world fell away until I could feel only my body—but I had no control. I felt everything happening to it, and could do nothing by take it. Each slam rocked me back and forth over the ridged cock. My body relaxed into it with a shiver. Discomfort became an instantaneous pleasure. I let it thrust wildly into me and loved it.

It was like I was realising my true purpose for the first time. All I was meant to be, all I was good for, was being this demon's slut. Its sex toy. Meat, a hole, nothing but this. Asmodeus would use me like a cock sleeve and fill me up, and I would *thank* it when it was over. Beg for it to do it again. Beg for it to use me until I couldn't be used at all.

My body writhed, and I grabbed the back of the prince's thighs and ground up into it. It sank into me until it was rolling its hips, balls slapping against my own with every movement. My hands quivered. I didn't want this slowness. I didn't want its teasing.

I said, "I'll never say another prayer to God in my life if

you fuck me hard. I want you. I want all of you. Make me a fucking mess."

Asmodeus' smile was slow and malevolent. "As you wish."

The pace quickened and then doubled until every slamming fuck was crushing my lungs. I screamed. Warm hands wrapped around my throat and pressed. No air—nothing but the devastating pressure. Hands crushing my windpipe. Lungs straining, then burning. Hands went limp at my sides as my body flopped around, moved only by the prince's cock. My eyes rolled. Vision began to blur—I was dying. I was going to be fucked to death. My straining cock quivered.

This was it. I was consumed by it—I was such a slut, just something to be used, and I loved it. With my life edging out of me, I had never felt closer to true bliss.

The pressure released, and I gasped raw and red. Air seared down my bruised throat—and the thrusting didn't stop.

"Take it," it roared at me. I was babbling beneath it. My feet bobbed pathetically. My moans pitched higher and higher. The demon thrusted, grip firm on my shoulder, grazing my prostate with every hard slam. I felt it in my stomach, felt it deep inside my body. Everything ached. Everything hurt. I was pulled roughly out of ecstasy into a screaming fear—I would die to this ruthless fuck.

"Please," I whispered.

I cried out, hands burying into Asmodeus' hair, pulling weakly at it, writhing, until I screamed, "*Mercy! Mercy, mercy, mercy.*"

It stopped. The suddenness frightened me. It dragged that wide, ridged cock out of me, and the emptiness was a shock. Sudden tears welled in my eyes.

"Mercy," Asmodeus repeated. It thumbed over my lips, leaned down, and kissed me. Its forked tongue levelled open my lips, licking at the tear its earlier slap had created. Then it slipped into me and moaned into my mouth. The kiss was heated, full, but gentle. I relaxed minutely under it.

"You're doing so well," it told me as it pulled away. "So, so well, little priest. Let yourself go."

"It hurts," I whispered.

"Yes," the prince told me. "But don't you love that?"

I shivered. I do. I do—I wanted the recklessness, the anger, the heat of violence. But I'm—

"Do not be frightened." The demon edged my chin up until I was craning to look at it. Then its hand wrapped around my cock. I thrusted up into its palm with a stilted moan—I was close to that touch. Oh—I had softened to Asmodeus. I soften to its wants. Its slow, determined strokes left me panting.

The Prince of Lust told me, "I do not want to kill you. I want to fuck you. I want to use you. Until you can't take it anymore. For eternity. Isn't that what you want?" Its voice turned to a whisper. "To be mine? Mine to use? Mine to *keep*?"

"Yes," I spoke involuntarily. Whatever Asmodeus unlocked in me was the thing answering. The basest desires. The filthiest wants. Yes. Yes. "I want to be yours."

My groan was low and long as the prince's cock slowly slid back into me. Every second stretched my hole, opening easily now to the demon's girth.

"That's it," Asmodeus murmured. It cooed at me, gently turning my face this way and that as it rolled forward. "Don't resist me. Don't hold back."

Its thrusts grew more insistent. More incessant. I let myself be fucked until I reached that place beyond the body again. Language left me. I was incoherent, blabbering nonsense, barely forming pleas and moans. A godly hymnic chant: *my prince, my prince, please.*

It fucked me harder, harder, faster, *faster,* and —

I arched as my body seized, ignited by the sudden orgasm that shuddered through my body. I fell limp; my soul was outside me, in Heaven, blessed and blinding white. But I was still in the demon's grip, and it didn't relent. It fucked my tired, listless body mercilessly, thrusting madly into my ass, and when I found my voice again and started mumbling, all cock-drunk and stupid, the demon shivered and came too.

All the demon's hot, built-up cum shot out into my eager body. Asmodeus groaned and threw its head back, exposing that graceful, tense neck. Its tail whipped around the stone room, unable to contain its ecstasy.

SEVEN

When it finally rolled forward, Asmodeus was still moaning keenly. It kept its softening cock deep in me as it leaned forward to kiss my neck. Sweat glistened off both our bodies. It put its head into my chest, a moment of vulnerable affection. Cautiously, I put my fingers into its hair. Smelt the cedar. The caramel. The sweat, the cum, the sex. Breathed it all in and felt—satisfied. For the first time in my life, there was no noise in my head.

"My little whore," Asmodeus growled from my chest. "My priestly slut. What a surprise you are."

It peeled its face from me and bared its sharp canine. Its fork tongue split around its teeth to lap at the sweat and cum smeared across my belly. I had nothing to say, and so the only noise that came out of me was a sigh.

"Fucked your thoughts away," the Prince of Lust commented. It pulled out of me unceremoniously and stood with its cock leaking. "You really are worthless, aren't you?"

I shivered and laid there. I didn't want to move. I didn't want to do anything that might dislodge the perfect moment.

"How will you live with yourself?" Asmodeus laughed.

I squeezed my eyes shut. *Don't think about tomorrow. Don't think about it.*

But the soft call of birds had already started somewhere beyond my small room. It wouldn't be long before the new bishop was summoned. Not long before the scroll was recorded missing, and I was marked as the culprit. Not long before I would be put to death for a myriad of crimes—for the sin of my lust. For the sin of partaking so happily in it.

Asmodeus tutted. "Don't look so despondent, little priest. There are plenty of cocks for you to bounce on."

I shifted and stared at it. "I thought I was yours."

The prince snorted. "In a sense. But whoring yourself out to anyone who looks at you is the proper way to worship me."

I sat up with a shiver. The shame of that—the nervous, excited thought of it—consumed me. Is that what I was now? Is that what I should do? Leave here, be used by whoever might want me?

"Have I sold my soul to you?" I whispered. God's anxious worry gnawing at my head.

Asmodeus looked down and toed the line of the pentagram with its foot. It glanced at me over its shoulder and ignored my question. "Do you plan to keep me, little priest?"

"What if I came with you?"

Asmodeus laughed again. "Ah. I didn't think it would happen so soon." When I said nothing, Asmodeus turned to me and tilted its head. "I've tasted you now. And you've tasted me. I can smell you. Feel you. I am an infection, little priest; I will destroy you from the inside out. Fill your core with rotten thoughts and let them fester for years until you open Hell itself and walk into it gladly. I do not need your soul. You will give it to me freely, just as you give your body."

I gulped. I blinked at it. "I can't wait years." My voice came out hoarse and frightened, but it was true. My body had learnt bliss after decades. Mortality is a curse; I didn't have eons to explore this. I didn't have millennia to whore myself. I had the moment. I had this life. I say again, slowly, "I can't wait years."

Asmodeus' smile held a dark, twisted glee. "I know," it says.

The unspoken thing passed between us: if I did not summon it again, I would find a way to go to it. I would worship it more keenly than I have worshipped God and with a feral need for it. I would walk gladly into Hell to taste it again. To be had by it again.

"But you cannot have me if you're caught now," Asmodeus murmured. "You can't have any of us."

"Us?"

"Plenty of demons in Hell," the prince said, sultry and slow. "My pathetic little priest."

Heat flooded me, but I got up.

"I . . ."

I didn't own Asmodeus. Not the way it owned me. In this sense, I knew I shouldn't have felt the way I did—like I was losing something. My stomach seized and I walked forward, pressing my hand against its chest.

Something akin to softness flared in the demon's eyes. "Missing me already?"

"Something like that."

A grin split those red lips apart, and sharp canines left indents against Asmodeus' lower lip. "Then let me leave you with a reminder," it said, and it went on its knees.

I jolted away as hot breath curled around my cock. But the demon's lip didn't part for me like that. Instead, it bared its teeth against my inner thigh—and bit.

I howled, slamming my hand against my mouth to smother the sound. Pain flared in a searing burst as teeth sank into my flesh, and I stumbled back against the bed, trying in vain to flee.

Asmodeus pulled away. My blood had stained its face and dribbled down its neck. "Hush, little priest," it cooed to me, licking my blood from its lips. "I'm just leaving my mark."

The Prince of Lust stood and assessed me. Sweat and panic had left me spread and quivering. Blood pooled down my inner thigh and onto the sheets. The puncture wounds ran deep. And they would scar.

"You'll think of me every time you see them," Asmodeus said with a grin. "Every time you touch yourself, I'll be there."

It leaned down, bracketing my hips with its clawed hands. Then it kissed me chastely. I tasted the metallic twang of my blood and gasped when it pulled away.

"Free me," it said. "Now."

I didn't want to. Believe me—the thought of blasphemy of a different kind curled in me. I wanted to trap the Prince of Lust there with me. Keep it in my room, use it the way I hoped it would use me.

I think Asmodeus knew what I was thinking because its eyes sparkled bright with amusement. It did not touch me again, and nor did it speak again. It waited to see what I would do. Whether I would obey it.

If I hadn't—if I'd trapped it there—I knew it would never fuck me again.

Which simply wouldn't do.

So, I moved. I followed that final order, and I rubbed the pentagram away.

Asmodeus smiled at me and nodded before it vanished into smoke.

I stood there and felt its absence. The air grew noticeably colder, and I shivered, first from the change in temperature and then from the growing abysmal knowledge that it would be some time before I saw it again.

But I would never see Asmodeus, Prince of Lust, again if I didn't manage to cover my tracks.

The only thing left to do was return the scroll, which I managed without issue. I burned the blood-covered sheets, went to mass that morning, prayed with my brethren, and waited for the bishop to come.

I did all these things with piety and faith—but not in the name of God.

Epilogue

This was how it all began.

In the end, without Asmodeus' presence, what keeps me going is the knowledge and the faith in it, faith of its return—and the certainty that I will see it again.

My eternity will be cock-filled. It will be demons. It will be burning for eternity in the heat of their breath and their cum.

But that is a glorious future. A much better life than piety in a dull abbey.

I belong to the Prince of Lust now. Completely.

And I pledge this:

I will learn how to open a gate to Hell.

About the Author

Lucien Burr has a background in the Classics and is an author and creator writing dark fantasy stories.

Also by Lucien Burr:

THE TERAS TRIALS

Printed in Great Britain
by Amazon